- KENNY LOGGINS -
FOOTLOOSE

ILLUSTRATED BY Tim Bowers

Music & Lyrics by Kenny Loggins & Dean Pitchford

SCHOLASTIC INC.

Zookeeper Big Jack
checks in his star map.
Tonight's a full moon.
Some **fun** is comin' soon.

All the **animals** are watchin'
to see if everyone's gone.
Gettin' ready to party,
they're gonna be **dancin'** till the dawn.

They're gonna cut loose.
Footloose!
Slip on their dancin' shoes.
Jeez, Louise,
rockin' the chimpanzees.

Jack, jump back!
Howlin' with the wolf pack.
Lose your blues.
Everybody cut Footloose!

Four llamas
all leap
while **lion's** tryin' to sleep.

Five rhinos in a row,
all jumpin', bumpin' to the
Mr. DJ Elephant's
funky, hip-hoppin' grooves.
Every monkey's out dancin',
giraffes and kangaroos are, too.

All the zoo's about to cut loose!
Footloose!
Slip on their dancin' shoes.
Ooh whee, **Marie**,
who's shakin' your tree?

Whoa, Milo,
teaching 'em all to tango.
Lose your blues.
Everybody cut Footloose!

First!
You got to turn me around.

Second!
And put your feet on the ground.

Third!
Do what the animals do.
They're turnin' it loose!

Footloose!

Slip on their dancin' shoes.

Ooh, Lulu,
what's that wiggle you do?

Jack,
jump back!
Here come the **ducks**, "quack, quack!"
Lose your blues.
Everybody cut **Footloose!**

Footloose!
Slip on your dancin' shoes.
Ooh whee, **Lucy**,
shake it, shake it for me.

Luke,
too cute,
funkiest cat in the zoo.
Lose your blues.
Everybody cut Footloose!

Footloose!
Slip on your dancin' shoes.
Oh, whoa, *here* ,
kickin' it heel to toe.

Jack,
don't nap.
The sunrise will soon be back.
But the zoo's
not through ...

Everybody cut, everybody cut.
Everybody cut, everybody cut.
Everybody cut, everybody cut.
**Everybody,
everybody cut Footloose!**

This is dedicated to my children and our ever-expanding clan.
I'm very proud of each and every one of you and excited to be "Pops"
to all of your children, too. —K.L.

To my granddaughter, Brylie. —T.B.

Performer's Note

In the summer of 1982, my good friend and co-lyricist Dean Pitchford asked me to check out
a screenplay he'd been writing called *Footloose*. As a favor to Dean I cowrote two songs
for his little movie project. In the long run it turned out to be a big favor to me when *Footloose*
became the biggest movie of the summer of 1984. (We didn't see that coming!)
The '80s also saw the beginning of my family. My first son, Crosby, was born in 1980,
and I had four more children over the next sixteen years.

Last year, Crosby and his wife, Brooke, had my first grandchild, Phifer, and my chance
to be the party-time troubadour has happily reemerged. Some of my best memories of being
a dad are singing with my kids, so it was only natural that I take "Footloose" and turn it into
a dance party for my new granddaughter . . . and 100 of her closest animal friends.

I hope this is as much fun for you and your children
as it has been for me to make and share with mine.

Illustrator's Note

I watch my little granddaughter dance. As soon as the music starts,
she dips and sways to the beat. Spin. Kick. Swirl. The room becomes a dance floor.
For years, people have been spinning, kicking, and swirling to Kenny Loggins' songs,
and now a new generation will feel the beat. I tried to capture that energy in my artwork.
Color. Shape. Texture. This newest version of "Footloose" visits the zoo.
Each turn of a page invites us to join the animals on the dance floor,
and we get another chance to put on our dancin' shoes.

ISBN 978-1-338-29905-2

12 11 10 9 8 7 6 5 4 3 2 1   18 19 20 21 22 23

Printed in the U.S.A.   08

First Scholastic printing, April 2018

About the Authors

Singer-songwriter Kenny Loggins has sold more than 25 million albums worldwide, has won two Grammy Awards, and co-wrote the book *The Unimaginable Life: Lessons Learned on the Path of Love.* His songs have been hits over the last four decades, including "This Is It," "I'm Alright," "Footloose," "Danger Zone," and so many more. In addition to his string of successful recordings, both solo and as a member of the famed duo Loggins & Messina, Kenny became the first major rock star to dedicate himself to recording music for children and families. His album *Return to Pooh Corner* remains the best-selling children's album of the last twenty years. Kenny, who reunited with Jim Messina in 2009, currently resides in Santa Barbara, CA.

Dean Pitchford, an American songwriter, screenwriter, director, actor, and novelist, has won an Oscar and a Golden Globe Award and has been nominated for three additional Oscars, two more Golden Globes, eight Grammy Awards, and two Tony Awards. His books, stage shows, and movies have earned an international following, and his songs have sold over 70 million records.

About the Illustrator

Tim Bowers has illustrated more than thirty-five children's books, including the *New York Times* best seller *Dream Big, Little Pig!*, written by Kristi Yamaguchi, and *Dinosaur Pet*, written by Neil Sedaka and Marc Sedaka. Although Tim grew up around unusual pets, including his grandparents' squirrel monkey and a singing African grey parrot, he never had pets that would dance. But he definitely wanted them to. He and his wife live in Granville, OH.